Baby Elephant's
Fun in the Sun

Parent's Introduction

This book can be read with children in several different ways. You can read the book to them or, depending on their ability, they may be able to read the book to you. You can also take turns reading! Throughout the book you will find words and phrases in big, bold text. If your child is just beginning to read, you might want to invite your child to participate in reading this text.

Your child may enjoy several readings of this story. With each reading, your child might see or focus on something new. As you read together, consider taking time to discuss the story and the information about the animals. At the end of the story, we have also included some fun questions to talk over together.

Baby Elephant's Fun in the Sun
A Photo Adventure™ Book

Concept, text and design Copyright © 2008 Q2AMedia.
Additional concepts, text and design Copyright © 2009 Treasure Bay, Inc.
Photo Adventure is a trademark of Treasure Bay, Inc. Patent No. 5,957,693.

Author	Michael Teitelbaum
Editor	Elizabeth Bennett
Publishing Director	Chester Fisher
Art Director	Sumit Charles
Designers	Joita Das and Rati Mathur
Project Managers	Ravneet Kaur and Shekhar Kapur
Art Editor	Sujatha Menon
Picture Researcher	Shweta Saxena

Picture Credits
t=top b=bottom c=centre l=left r=right m=middle
Front Cover SouWest Photography/ Shutterstock; Back Cover: Alan Weaving / AfriPics.com; Half Title: Mitch Reardon/ Photolibrary; 3 Martin Harvey/ NHPA; 4-5 Martyn Colbeck/ Photolibrary; 5tr Victor Soares/ Istockphoto; 6 RICHARD DU TOIT/ Naturepl; 7b Steve & Ann Toon/ Photolibrary; 8-9 Nigel J Dennis/ Photolibrary; 9m Mitch Reardon/ Photolibrary; 10-11 Peter Adams/ GettyImages; 11m Peter Blackwell/ Naturepl; 12 Steffen Foerster Photography/ Shutterstock; 14 Alan Weaving / AfriPics.com; 15b Mikaela/ Shutterstock; 16-17 Martyn Colbeck/ OSF/ Photolibrary; 18-19 Heinrich van den Berg/ GettyImages; 20-21 Ann and Steve Toon / Alamy; 22-23 Michael K. Nichols/ Gettyimages; 23t Tony Camacho/ Science photolibrary/ Photolibrary; 24 James Warwick/ GettyImages

Published by Treasure Bay, Inc.
40 Sir Francis Drake Boulevard
San Anselmo, CA 94960 USA

PRINTED IN SINGAPORE

Library of Congress Catalog Card Number: 2008934735

Hardcover ISBN-10: 1-60115-283-3
Hardcover ISBN-13: 978-1-60115-283-1
Paperback ISBN-10: 1-60115-284-1
Paperback ISBN-13: 978-1-60115-284-8

Visit us online at:
www.TreasureBayPublishing.com

A big herd of elephants roams the grasslands of Africa.

So many **elephants!**

3

4

Elephants are the biggest land animals in the world.

Baby Elephant is part of this herd. She stands near her mother.

Baby Elephant eats leaves and **grass.**

5

Baby Elephant is thirsty.
She leans down to get
a drink of **water.**

Elephants learn to use
their trunks to help
them drink.

7

The sun is **hot,**
but Baby Elephant stays cool.

She finds a shady **spot** next to her mother.

FACT STOP

A baby elephant starts to walk just one hour after it is born!

9

It is playtime! And Baby Elephant loves to **play.**

She chases birds.

Fly away, **birds!**

FACT STOP

Sometimes, baby elephants butt their heads in play.

12

Look at that vine!

To pick it up, Baby Elephant
uses her **trunk.**

14

Baby Elephant has lots of friends.
She loves to play with her friends.

They love to roll around
in the **mud.**

FACT STOP

Elephants roll in
mud to stay
cool.

15

Baby Elephant and her friends push each other as they **play.**

This helps them get strong.

17

Time for a **bath!**

Baby Elephant splashes
in the water.

Baby Elephant is having **lots of fun** playing in the water.

Her mother says it is time to go, but Baby Elephant does not want to go.

21

Baby Elephant's aunt gives her a gentle push.

This means that it really is time to go. Baby Elephant hurries off with the rest of the herd.

Her playful day has come to an **end.**

You have two sets of teeth during your life. Elephants have six!

Look back

through the story:

1 What are some fun activities baby elephants do with their friends?

2 What do baby elephants like to eat?

3 How do baby elephants stay cool on a hot day?

4 When it is hot and sunny, what do you like to do?